The Carrot Cake Catastrophe!

For my daughter, Jenny, and her
Grandad, Charles, with much love
E.D.

For Grandad Joe and Nan Winnie,
who I know will be smiling down at
the catastrophe that this cake is
G.R.

This edition published by Parragon Books Ltd in 2013

Parragon Books Ltd
Chartist House
15–17 Trim Street
Bath BA1 1HA, UK

www.parragon.com

Published by arrangement with Gullane Children's Books

Text © Elizabeth Dale 2012
Illustrations © Gemma Raynor 2012

ISBN 978-1-4723-3197-7

Printed in China

The Carrot Cake Catastrophe!

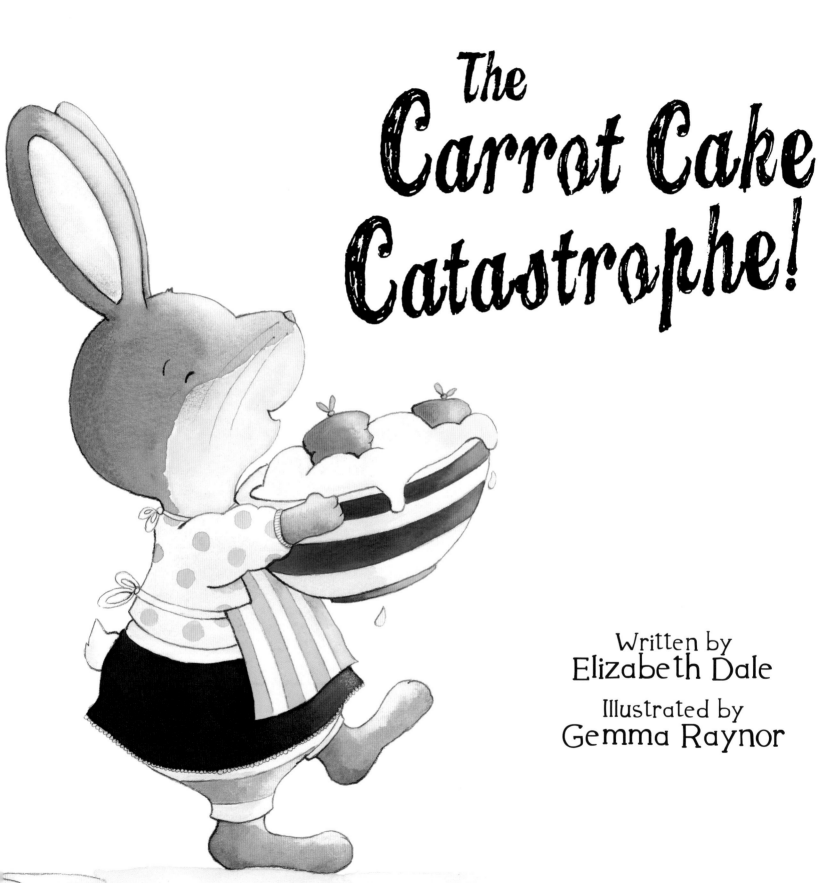

Written by
Elizabeth Dale

Illustrated by
Gemma Raynor

PaRragon

Bath • New York • Singapore • Hong Kong • Cologne • Delhi
Melbourne • Amsterdam • Johannesburg • Shenzhen

Jenny was very excited.
Today was her mummy's birthday and, while she was out,
Jenny and Grandad were planning a birthday surprise.

"Let's make a carrot cake!"

cried Jenny.

They found a carrot cake recipe in
Mummy's recipe book. It looked delicious.

"Can you read the big words for me, Grandad?"
asked Jenny. Grandad put on his glasses, the kind
that made writing clear, but everything else rather
blurry. "150 grams of **butter**," he read.

He peered round.
"Now, where's that butter...?"

300 gr
100 gram

150 grams
1 teaspoon grо

"What's next?" asked Jenny, scooping it into the bowl.
"150 grams of **flour**," read Grandad.

OH NO! Grandad grabbed...

... the icing sugar!
White clouds flew everywhere.
"**Oops!**" giggled Jenny.

Once Grandad had cleaned his glasses,
he reached for the recipe book.
"Now, 200 grams of **carrots**.

Yummy! Let's get digging..."

Jenny looked round the garden.
"How funny having vegetables in a cake!
Imagine a **brussels sprout** cake... or a **cabbage cake!**"
"No, thank you!" laughed Grandad. "I'll stick to carrot
cake any day and ours is going to be the
tastiest cake ever!"

Grandad and Jenny washed the carrots
and added them to the mixture, but...

OH NO! They
forgot to chop them!
"Oh dear," said Jenny, "it doesn't look quite right."

"We haven't stirred it yet!" said Grandad.
Jenny stirred and stirred.

"Next," said Grandad, "we need **walnuts**, then **eggs** and **caster sugar** and a teaspoon of **cinnamon**."

"Walnuts first..."

OH NO!
They went
in whole!

"Eggs next..."

OH NO!
Shells and all!

"Here's the sugar..."

OH NO!
Grandad reached for
the salt!

"Can't see anything
wrong with that now,"
said Grandad. "Can you?"

With Grandad's help, Jenny poured the mixture into two tins and then watched as Grandad put them carefully into the oven.

Jenny couldn't wait for the cake to be cooked.
Mummy was going to love it!

Finally the cake was done.
"OH NO!" said Jenny, "it doesn't look quite right!"
They each tried a crumb.
"OH NO!" said Grandad, "it doesn't taste quite right!
But we followed the recipe EXACTLY..."

"We forgot the cinna-thingy, that's why!" cried Jenny.
"And Mummy will be back any moment!"

QUICK!
Let's hide the cake...

"in the garden!"

When Mummy came in, Jenny was quiet.
"What's wrong, Jenny?" asked Mummy.
"We were making a birthday surprise
for you," said Jenny. "But it's a
catastrophe!"

And she led Mummy out
to the garden...

which was full of
beautiful birds!
"You've invited the birds
— how clever you are!"
said Mummy. "This is the
best birthday surprise EVER!"

Jenny and Grandad exchanged a secret smile.
"And I've made a surprise for you too," said Mummy.
"Can you guess what it is?"

"It's a carrot cake!"
cried Jenny.
"It's a good job we gave ours to
the birds," Grandad whispered.

"Who wants a slice?" asked Mummy.
"I do!" cried Jenny and Grandad.

"Happy birthday!"

Carrot Cake

Cake Ingredients

150 g butter

150 g caster sugar

2 eggs, beaten

1 tsp vanilla essence

300 g grated carrots

100 g finely chopped walnuts

150 g flour

1 tsp baking powder

1 tsp bicarbonate of soda

1 tsp ground cinnamon

Icing Ingredients

150 g cream cheese

50 g icing sugar

grated zest of half an orange

Recipe to be used under the direct supervision of an adult.

Method

Pre-heat the oven to 180°C / Gas 4.

In a large bowl, beat the butter and sugar together until light and fluffy.

Beat the eggs into the mixture. Stir in the carrots, walnuts, vanilla essence and cinnamon.

Sift the flour, baking powder and bicarbonate of soda, and fold gently into the mixture.

Pour into two 18-cm cake tins and cook for 30 minutes. Turn cakes out onto a rack and allow to cool.

To make the icing, spoon the cream cheese and orange zest into a bowl.

Sift in the icing sugar and beat until smooth. Spread half of the icing on top of first cake tier.

Place the second tier on top, spreading with the remaining icing.